A Long Way from the Road

The Wit and Wisdom of Prince Edward Island

David Weale

with illustrations by
Dale McNevin

Charlottetown
1998

A Long Way from the Road:
The Wit and Wisdom of Prince Edward Island

Editor: Laurie Brinklow
Designer: Jane Ledwell

Printed and bound in Canada

10 9 8 7 6 5 4

Canadian Cataloguing in Publication Data

Weale, David, 1942 —

A long way from the road

ISBN 0-9698606-3-3

1. Prince Edward Island — Social life and customs — Anecdotes. I. Title.

FC2618.W418 1998 971.7 C98-950245-7
F1047.W418 1998

Published by
The Acorn Press
P.O. Box 22024
Charlottetown, Prince Edward Island
C1A 9J2

A Long Way from the Road

THERE ARE ADVANTAGES TO living in an out-of-the-way place like Prince Edward Island. Our insularity, however inconvenient, has always permitted the emergence of native peculiarity, and the idiomatic texturing of character and imagination. It's what I love about the place. But as every corner of the world becomes more and more a cultural franchise of mainstream America, that distinctiveness becomes increasingly blurred, and its survival increasingly threatened. We find we are not such a long way from the road after all.

It is perhaps naive to believe that the birthright of vernacular wit and wisdom might somehow withstand the powerful levelling forces of the modern age, and that we might actually be able to survive as a crooked little people, living on our crooked little Island, with our own crooked little sense of humour. But I do believe it's worth the effort, and this book, rich with the stories and voices of many Islanders, is dedicated to that survival.

Contents

ACKNOWLEDGEMENTS

Many readers will recognize their stories in this collection, and I am grateful you shared them with me; however, when I began compiling the material, I realized immediately that acknowledging my sources was going to be a problem. Because the stories have been accumulating in my mind and in my files for more than twenty-five years, I simply cannot remember where many of them originated. Further, I am aware that many of my sources might not wish to be identified, as was expressed in the following quotation from an informant:

> When Aunt Florence [name changed] died, Hughie [name changed] and I went to the casket and the first thing we noticed was how dirty her fingernails were. And for God's sake don't say this on the radio. Some of her family members are still living.

Because it seemed an impossible task to decide who I should or should not acknowledge, I decided in the end to exclude references to individual informants and simply thank anonymously the hundreds of Islanders, living and dead, who have contributed to the making of this book, and without whose collaboration it could not have been written.

My informants will also recognize that, in many instances, I have exercised my prerogative as a storyteller in the embellishing and embroidering of many of the anecdotes. Few are exactly as I heard them. An Island man told me once that a good storyteller had the knack of "putting a new coat" on a story. I confess to having attempted much of that in this collection, and accept full responsibility for any errors or misrepresentations resulting from my "dressing-up" of the material.

My special thanks to my publisher, Laurie Brinklow; to Dale McNevin for her evocative illustrations, which are a story in themselves; to Anna Fisher, who makes difficult tasks seem easy; to Alan Buchanan, who was the first to tell me the title story; and to Ed MacDonald, who read the manuscript, made some helpful suggestions, and endorsed the project with his laughter.

INTRODUCTION

"DESPERATE FUNNY"

"Oh he was terrible witty Tom was,
oh desperate altogether."
— Jimmy Doyle,
Alberry Plains

From one tip of Prince Edward Island to the other, the burden of existence has always been lightened by the droll humour and funny stories that are the standard fare of daily conversation. In a society that was often difficult, even grim, humour was the saving grace: a seasoning of mirth which made life more palatable. Along with the hard work and deep faith, it was the omnipresent laughter that made survival possible. There were many lean times, but we had our own stories, and there was a richness in that.

And what do we laugh about here on the Island? Well, pretty much the same things people laugh about everywhere else. About being poor and mean and afraid; about sex and politics and the fear of death; about insecurity, incapacity, and imbecility. In short, about being mortal human beings. That's not to say there is no difference in Island humour. Islanders laugh at the same things, but in their own offbeat and offshore manner. And sometimes we just plain laugh at who we are — at being Islanders.

The stories collected for this volume amuse me greatly, but there is more to it than that. I have also discovered there is no better way to discern the heart and soul of a people than by paying attention to what makes them laugh. The life of a society can be investigated and documented by historians, or sociologists, or even by folklorists, but for those with the ears to hear, it is the humour that best exposes the inner landscape of communal experience. There is a common saying that we "break into laughter," and it is in that "breaking" that we catch a brief glimpse of the hidden underside of the individual and the community. The word "wisecrack" suggests a similar disclosure. Joseph Campbell once said about myth that it "opens backwards into the deep mystery of things." It is the same with humour. Listen carefully to the laughter and you will detect more than what meets the ear. There is always something breaking through.

Islanders often use the phrase, "desperate funny." It is a most perceptive colloquialism, for surely there is always some element of desperation in humour. We call it the "light side," but the connection to the "dark "is clearly suggested. Humour almost always has its roots in the subsoil of anxiety where exist those fears and tensions too dreadful to discuss openly, but, fortunately, not too dreadful to laugh about. It's why we sometimes laugh until we weep, and why many older Islanders have the saying, "Laugh, I nearly cried." You might even say that we don't so much laugh because we're happy, but because we wish to be, or, as William Blake once noted, "Excess of sorrow laughs."

Laughter is soul work — an everyday sacrament of confession, exorcism, and expiation all rolled into one. It is the creative exhalation and venting of pent-up tension that otherwise can deform the spirit, or explode with devastating results. One day at the rink I overheard two men in a terrible argument. Finally, the most aggrieved individual said, "I'm right at the place where this can go either way."

"What do you mean?" demanded the other.

"I'm either going to have to laugh this off," replied the first, "or break your goddamned neck." The two of them then "broke" into laughter and harm was averted — at least for a time.

At its worst, of course, humour can be a means of chronic deferral; a way of refusing to come to terms with the root causes of pain and distress. So it's not altogether flattering that jocularity is such a prominent part of our culture. There's a sense in which too much humour is no laughing matter. But who can judge such a thing? We laugh because we must, and surely a community that can't laugh at itself becomes a place of many hidden dangers. Perhaps in becoming aware of those things that make us laugh again and again, we can become more aware of those things that make us most afraid.

I have also observed that humour is often a camouflage for criticism and invective. In this tightly knit province of neighbours and relatives, where grudge-holding is endemic, it is often not wise to criticize or protest openly. Sly humour is a less hazardous form of disagreement, and the "wisecrack" a compromise between saying too much and saying nothing at all.

I have made no attempt in this collection to identify or categorize the humour according to ethnic origin. That is a job for the ethnologist. It is a matter of only incidental concern to me whether the humour is Irish, Scottish, or Acadian. My own view is that there has been a long blending and mingling of traditions into a single identity and that, as a consequence, the humour presented in this volume is best described as Island humour.

I also am not, strictly speaking, a folklorist. The academic discipline of folklore is concerned with preserving exactly what was said and locating it as precisely as possible within the historical timeframe. The tradition of storytelling, on the other hand, is about borrowing, adapting, embellishing, and re-telling within the ongoing life of the community. I have done a lot of that in this book.

But enough analysis. I could have written a much longer introduction, but am a firm believer that while it is possible to discuss a potato, it does more good to eat it. So let's get on to the stories, and whether your laugh is hard and sardonic, like a thrown stone, or gurgly-soft, like brook-song; whether it's one of those reserved, stuttery laughs, like the sound of one of those old single-piston engines, or a great fulsome belly-shaker that puts you completely out of control, I hope this book will draw it out of you. May you discover for yourself the alchemy of the stories, able to transform the heavy metals of human predicament into the lightness of laughter — the helium of good humour.

And if you laugh 'til you cry, so much the better.

A Long Way from the Road

THIS IS AN ISLAND of characters, men and women of no great fame who achieved local notoriety for their wit and wisdom and the esoteric charm of their eccentricity. They never bore the title, but many of them were actually trickster figures, able to deflate the overly serious and pious pretensions of their neighbours with the deft barb of humourous insight. People chuckled at their antics, and laughed at their stories, often not realizing they were laughing at themselves.

Harry MacTavish of Belfast was such a character. A legendary wit, with a quicksilver tongue, Harry was the resident master of the one-liner. I have heard many tales about him, but my favourite is the one about the two travelling evangelists.

It appears there were these two soldiers of the Lord — oh! terribly earnest chaps — who were going house-to-house trying to save the locals. They arrived at last at Harry's place, located up the end of a very long lane. Now Harry, who was probably no more or less Christian than most of his neighbours, saw them coming, and invited them into his home. There, Bible opened, they were able to share with him for some time the merits of their particular doctrine. It was all very cordial.

It soon became clear, however, that they really weren't getting anywhere with Harry, who seemed more bemused than convicted. Finally, with more than just a touch of exasperation, one of them blurted, "Mr. MacTavish, do you not realize that Jesus died for your sins?"

There was a long pause.

"Nooo," replied Harry, "Nooo, I didn't. You see, I'm a long way from the road."

The Map

I REMEMBER WELL THE schoolhouse in Greenmount, just up the hill from the church. It was one of those austere, primitive little buildings with a steep-pitched roof, and windows along either side. Inside the decor was definitely minimalist. It had a worn-shiny spruce board floor, several rows of badly scarred double desks, and in the middle a big black woodstove with an eccentric stovepipe, held up with wires, which zigged and zagged its way through the air and somehow made it out through the roof. There was little to suggest we were in the middle of the twentieth century.

At the front was the teacher's desk, with a Bible in one drawer, and a strap in the other, and on one wall a large, Jersey Milk map of the world, with all the possessions of the British Empire coloured boldly in Imperial red. I remember standing in front of that map with a little friend looking for Prince Edward Island and feeling just a little bit anxious. I knew the Island was small and was afraid it wouldn't be on the map.

It reminds me of a story a friend told me. One day he and a buddy were acting up pretty bad in school. Finally, the exasperated teacher marched down to their seats, grabbed them by the ears and fairly hoisted the two of them into the air. She proceeded to administer a tongue-lashing, but right in the middle of her tirade she looked over and saw diligent little Chester standing in front of the map, his face pressed up close somewhere in the vicinity of China.

"Look there," she said, "why can't you two be like Chester. Here you are wasting your time, and look at him, broadening his mind."

Chester, of course, heard all of this and swelled right up with pride.

"And what great part of the world are you looking for today?" she asked him.

"Please teacher," he replied, "I'm lookin' for Savage Harbour."

The Return

One thing we certainly do possess on the Island is a powerful sense of place, and a deep attachment to home. Whether it's the place you're leaving with wanderlust in your blood, or the one you're coming back to with arthritis in your joints, the Island is a most emphatic geographic and psychological reality — its dear, queer shape imprinted forever on your brain.

Over the years, many Islanders have moved away, but most come back sooner or later. Some, like salmon, come back to die. Just recently an Islander said to me, "David, the reason the population of the Island has increased so much in recent years is that so many Islanders come home to die . . . and don't."

Others come swinging back year after year on their great annual pilgrimage. The geese and the smelt come back in April; the relatives in July and August.

An old friend told me once about the compulsion of this return migration of Islanders. He recounted with a twinkle in his eye the story of the Island woman who died and went to heaven. As it was her first time there, she was being given a guided tour of the Celestial City by none other than St. Peter himself. It was everything she had hoped for. There were pearly gates, crystal fountains, streets paved with gold — and lupins in all the ditches. Everyone was having a wonderful, heavenly time.

However . . . as she rounded a turn she encountered a most disconcerting sight — something you would not expect to see in Paradise. In front of her was a large metal cage, and, inside, a group of unhappy people staring disconsolately between the bars.

"Who are they, for heaven's sake?" she asked in surprise.

"Oh!" replied St. Peter rather sheepishly, "they're from the Island. If we let them out they all try to go back."

Native Stone

ISLANDERS HAVE AN INCURABLE tendency to divide the entire population of the world into two groups: those from here, and those from "away." It amuses some visitors and irritates others. But there is no offense intended. It's just one of those idiosyncracies arising naturally from our insularity.

A former Premier of the province used to tell the story of the elderly Island woman who was admitted to the hospital for day surgery. Her physician asked her if she would be satisfied with a local anaesthetic. She pondered for a moment. "I suppose that would be all right," she replied hesitantly, "but are they as well-trained as the ones from away?"

I also learned very early that, in the minds of some Islanders, belonging to the Island is not a matter of residency, but of birth; not a matter of choice, but of conception. Indeed, I've heard it said that an Islander — a true Islander — is someone conceived above the high-water mark.

In one location up-west, there are some very large granite boulders strewn about, which look strikingly out-of-place on this otherwise granite-free, sandstone Island. Years ago, a man from the vicinity was asked about them. "It's like this," he said. "They're not really Island stones. They were dragged here by the glacier."

Never Heard of It

A MAN FROM UP-EAST enlisted in the Merchant Navy. His ship put in at New York and when he went ashore he struck up a conversation on the pier with a native New Yorker. The man, a stevedore, asked him where he was from. "Prince Edward Island," he replied.

The New Yorker shook his head. "Never heard of it," he said.

"That's funny," responded the Islander, a little taken aback, "everyone on Prince Edward Island has heard of New York."

It's just a fact of life, when you live on a small, out-of-the-way island, you almost always know more about other places than the people there know about you. But not always.

A farmer from the Fort Augustus area, nicknamed Din, was known locally for his great lack of education. He was, apparently, a man with a great sonorous voice who spoke desperate slow. One day he was talking to a neighbour about a vessel docked at Cranberry Wharf on the Hillsborough River. Din asked him if he had heard about Len Ferguson, then proceeded with his story. "Yesterday," he recounted, "Len hauled two loads of potatoes down to the wharf and boarded 'em all by hisself. Quite a thing."

The neighbour nodded agreement, then asked where the vessel was bound for. "Nova Scotia," drawled Din, "wherever the hell that is."

But then again, Din is the same fellow who is alleged to have asked a returned veteran if it was him or his twin brother who had been killed in the war.

Cavendish

A YOUNG MAN FROM Albany was a student at Mount Allison University in the 1970s and always worked summers on the boat at Borden. One day, over lunch, he was talking to an older man who had worked on the ferries for more than thirty years and was retiring that fall. To keep the conversation going, he asked him what he was going to do then, and the older man informed him that he and his wife were planning a trip. "Where are you headed?" he asked, thinking they were probably going to Boston, or maybe out west, or somewhere like that.

The man, without a hint of guile, informed him they were going to Cavendish.

"Cavendish?" he replied incredulously, thinking maybe he had misunderstood.

"Yes," replied the ferry worker, "I been hearin' the tourists talk about that place for thirty years, and now I plan on goin' up there and seein' it for myself."

Pure Islanders

An old-timer was asked if he had lived on the Island all his life. "No," he replied stiffly, "not yet." It puts me in mind of the two brothers — twins — who lived in Dromore, a place so out-of-the-way that even most Islanders couldn't tell you where it is. As old men, these two, Jimmie and Joe, were still living in the same little house in which they had been born, so an acquaintance decided one day to ask if they had ever been off the Island.

"I was to Nova Scotia once on a gravel truck," replied Jimmie, "but the damn thing broke down and we had to spend the night away. And I can tell ya, I was some glad to get back."

"And what about you, Joe?" he asked the other brother. "You ever been off the Island?"

"No," replied Joe. "I never was across. But it's all right, boy. It's all right. I like it better here anyway."

Another old gentleman, from High Bank, was equally limited in his travels, and when he was an old man it was widely rumoured in his home area that he had never been to Guernsey Cove, a community so close he doubtless had often seen it from the top of his barn. A man who had known him all his life remarked to me, "I hope there's a heaven, because it's the only way Lem is ever going to get off the Island."

Born Here

It was many years ago, fifty, perhaps even sixty, but even back then there were many summer visitors driving the little back roads of the Island, all agog over the Arcadian beauty of the place.

For the locals it was a novelty to see all the foreigners in their shiny cars and city clothes appearing in their little communities where, throughout the rest of the year, they knew most everybody who went up, and everybody who went down. But the visitors weren't unwelcome. It gave the country people something different to talk about, and it helped that the strangers all seemed so taken with the place.

One such visitor, travelling somewhere in back of Wood Islands, rolled up in a cloud of dust to where a farmer was working in the field stacking hay. Seeking directions, he went over to the fence and struck up a conversation, during which he commented fulsomely on the beauty of the day and the charm of the landscape. He was intrigued by the rustic, dour old gentleman, who reminded him of the peasants he had read about in one of Tolstoy's novels. The old man seemed as much a part of the scene before him as the coils of hay, the longer fence, and the spruce trees along the hedgerow. As they chatted, he wondered to himself about the man's education, and whether he had ever been anywhere else. Finally he asked the farmer if he had travelled much.

"No," replied the old man most deliberately, "I didn't have to. I was born here."

No Signal Needed

CONTRARY TO CONVENTIONAL WISDOM, Islanders are not especially bad drivers, they just have their own homebred rules of the road. These rules, however, can astound and sometimes infuriate visitors to the province who expect us to conform to their preconceived ideas of proper highway decorum. They come upon two vehicles stopped side by side on the highway, with the drivers chatting through open windows, and immediately assume there is something wrong with the picture. They don't understand it's a well-established local custom, and that if you wait patiently they will eventually move. Eventually.

A visitor was driving down a busy highway, following a car with Island plates. The pace was a little too slow for him, so he pulled out to pass, but no sooner did he get into the passing lane than the Island car cut across in front of him and onto a little unpaved secondary road. Well, the visitor got a terrible fright, and it made him frightful cross; so cross, in fact, that he wheeled around and took off after the Island car, all the while waving for the driver ahead to pull over.

The Island man finally noticed all this and pulled over to one side. The two men stepped out of their vehicles and the shaken visitor proceeded to give the Island man a piece of his mind. "That was a stupid trick," he shouted. "Have you never discovered your signal lights?"

The Island man was quite taken aback by the vehemence. Islanders, of course, are not nearly so direct with their insults. But it didn't take him long to get his feet under him. "Look Mister," he said, "I'm sorry, and I can see you're pretty upset. But I've got to tell ya, my people have lived on this road for four generations. Everyone knows I always turn in here."

A Year Like This

IN THE DAYS BEFORE rock stars and sports heroes there were work heroes, on every farm, in every boat, and in every kitchen: men and women renowned for their ability to work long and work hard. Male or female, there was no greater compliment than to be known as "a good worker." It was a source of great personal satisfaction, but it also resulted in a fair amount of grumbling. You couldn't whinge and whine too much — that wasn't acceptable — but the strain on body and soul of unremitting labour had to be expressed somehow, and often it crept out in the humour.

A farmer from just outside Summerside went to town every now and then to get his hair cut. He was one of those inveterate grumblers who never had anything good to say about farming. If it wasn't the bad weather it was the poor crops, and if it wasn't the poor crops it was the low prices. The barber heard it all, over and over, this litany of misfortune, and commiserated as any good barber will.

But then came one of those exceptional years. Everything was grand: the weather was beautiful, the crops bountiful, and the prices up. There was, it seemed, little cause for complaint. The mischievous barber, attempting to get the man to admit, just for once, to his good fortune, reminded him just what a great year it had been.

"Well yes," the farmer muttered, "it's been pretty good I suppose. But don't you know, a year like this . . . takes an awful lot out of the land."

This Is the Roads Boy

BEFORE THE INTERNAL COMBUSTION engine made its noisy and bumptious appearance on the farms and in the boats, the ability to endure long hours of brute physical labour was the key to survival. Indeed, it wouldn't be stretching it to say that in that "sweat of the brow" economy, hard manual labour was regarded as intrinsically virtuous, and the tendency to avoid it a sure sign of defective character.

Those raised in that regime expected hard labour, and one man recounted how shocking it was when he found himself in a situation where the esteemed work ethic seemed not to apply. "I remember my first week workin' on the roads in the 40s," he recalled. "Everything was mud, and almost everything had to be done either by hand or with a horse and cart."

After he had slaved away for several days, an old guy, a veteran of the roadcrew, sidled up with some strange advice, delivered out the corner of his mouth.

"This is the roads, boy," he said. "Ya don't hafta work that hard."

A Savin' Woman

On Prince Edward Island the virtue of hard work had a twin. It was the virtue of frugality. Oh my, yes! Frugality was like a religion. It couldn't save your soul, but it inspired you to save just about everything else. And, as with all religion, there were some Islanders who were fanatics, like the old Scot who advised his son to take his glasses off when he wasn't actually looking at anything.

In Summerside, after one of the stage performances of "A Long Way from the Road," a woman approached me in the lobby of the Jubilee Theatre. "David," she said with a great smile, "have I got a story for you" — words I always delight in hearing. She proceeded to tell me that in her family they all knew their grandmother was a "savin' person," but didn't realize how savin' until after she died. A few days after her funeral they were sorting through her things and discovered, up on a shelf, a most remarkable item. On the side of a small box the old woman had placed a label, and on the label she had printed neatly: PIECES OF STRING TOO SHORT TO SAVE.

The Mouse in the Buttermilk

A GOOD STORY HAS wings and is able to travel swiftly from one community to the next, or even from one country to the next. Further, stories with their genesis in one community were often adapted to fit the characters or circumstances of another. Most storytellers were quite shameless in this regard, believing correctly that some stories are just too good not to change.

The following yarn is a good example of this mobility and adaptation. I have no idea where it originated, but it is told in each of the three counties of the Island as though it happened there.

An old woman arrived at the merchant's store one morning with a sizeable "junk" of butter. She took him aside and explained that when she finished churning she had discovered a dead mouse in the buttermilk. "There's not a thing in the world wrong with the butter," she insisted, "but my family found out and now they won't touch it." She then asked him if she could trade it for another piece and suggested he could sell hers to someone else. "What they don't know won't hurt them," she concluded slyly.

The merchant, an obliging man, said it sounded like a good idea. He took her butter out back where she couldn't see him and pounded it into a different shape, then took his butter knife and squared it off at the ends. Arriving back at the counter, he whispered confidentially, "You're in luck. I found a piece just about the same size. I'll sell yours to someone else and, like you say, what they don't know won't hurt them."

Too Mean

A MAN UP ALBANY way was well known for holding on tightly to every penny and putting the death-grip on every dollar. He was an individual who would have been described as "mean" or "tight" — one of those creatures who just can't let go of anything.

The people in that culture had never heard of Sigmund Freud, but they knew all about anal retentiveness, and had some wonderfully clever and down-to-earth ways of describing the anal personality. Such an individual was "as tight as a frog's ass underwater," "as tight as a bull's ass in flytime," or "too mean to shit away from home."

They're crude, and lewd, but they do capture the mood.

But back to the story. The tight old geezer had managed, by the end of his life, to gather together quite a tidy sum of money, which was a source of aggravation to one of his neighbours. It irked him that the old man had no electricity, no phone, and no inside plumbing.

One day the neighbour decided he should speak out. "Fred," he said, "don't you think it's time you got some good out of your money? For God's sake man, you'll soon be dead, then someone else is going to get it and spend it all."

It was a delicate moment, but the old man held his ground.

"You're probably right," he said, "you're probably right. I can only hope they get as much pleasure out of spendin' it as I did out of holdin' on to it."

Bibles and Beads

RELIGIOUS BIGOTRY WAS PART of the baggage our European forebears brought with them to this place. Protestants and Roman Catholics settled side by side, in Rose Valley and Kinkora, in Glen Martin and St. Mary's Road, in Alberton and Tignish; and for two hundred years virtually every aspect of life in this province has been coloured by that proximity. Friendship and goodwill often prevailed over ancient prejudices, but it was always a factor to be reckoned with, and it was difficult for a Protestant to view a Roman Catholic, or vice versa, without looking through the spectacles of inherited bias.

My Protestant childhood provided me with a considerable arsenal of negative stereotypes of Roman Catholics. The most repeated slur against them was that they "worshipped Mary." This, more than anything else, seemed a sure sign of the degradation of their spiritual vision. Fifty years later I have some insight into why Protestants so feared this "Mariolatry," but back then it was simply dismissed as egregious error. It was beyond discussion — but not beyond humour.

A Catholic man and a Protestant man were walking together along a road somewhere near Morell. The Catholic man was all bent out of shape over something or other, and finally couldn't hold it in any longer. "Holy Everlastin' Mother of God," he exclaimed vehemently.

Well! The Protestant man was deeply offended. "I don't know why you call her holy?" he remonstrated, "she's no different than my own mother."

"Perhaps not," replied the Catholic man, "perhaps not. But quite a difference in the boys."

Too Bad He's Protestant

IT WAS CONFUSING WHEN Protestants discovered that Roman Catholics weren't the devils they expected them to be. The very foundations of their world view shook a little when that happened. It was, of course, the same on the other side, and I smiled when a Catholic friend told me recently that, as a child, he would often hear the old people say, "Great man. Too bad he's Protestant."

Some, of course, were more prejudiced than others, like the old fella in Charlottetown, a trucker, who hauled coal around the city in his horse and cart. He was a staunch member of Zion Presbyterian Church, and a rank supporter of the Liberal party — not an uncommon combination.

It was the early 1960s, and being such a congenital Liberal it was a matter of great distress to him that so many Islanders were caught up in the Diefenbaker-mania of the times. John Diefenbaker was the Conservative Prime Minister of the country, and a man who gained the adulation and respect of many in this province, including some Liberals. But not the man from Zion.

During one election campaign, Diefenbaker, "The Chief," came to Charlottetown for a rally. It was an enormous success, and I know for a fact there were old-timers attended from up-west who had never before been east of Borden. The next day the papers were filled with it, and a friend of the trucker decided it was a good chance to get a rise out of him.

"Well George," he said, "what do you think of Diefenbaker today? Quite a man, wouldn't you say!"

George's face twisted into a terrible grimace. "I hate him," he said, "I hate him with all my heart. I only wish he was Catholic so I could hate him more."

What's in a Name?

It happened when I was twelve or thirteen. A group of us had been transported to Charlottetown from Summerside on the train to take part in the annual spring music festival. We didn't get to Charlottetown very often in those days, so a friend and I decided it was a shame to waste the day hanging around the auditorium at Prince of Wales College waiting our turn to sing. The allure of uptown was just too powerful, so we set off on our great adventure.

The first spot we landed was Woolworth's on Queen Street. They had jelly doughnuts there, and a little booth just inside the door where you could have your picture taken four times for a quarter. I've since lost those pictures, but I'll never forget what happened next.

Somehow we ended up on the sidewalk in front of St. Dunstan's Basilica, staring up awe-struck at the mighty steeples which seemed to extend halfway to the clouds. Neither of us had ever seen anything like it before, and we knew in our boy-hearts that the opportunity could not be wasted. We must go inside.

We opened the massive door slowly and peered into the vestibule. It was empty. Good! Emboldened, we peeked through the inside doors into the church itself. Oh my! It was awesome, with statues peering down, candles flickering, and sunlight slanting in through the windows and around the great columns. Our hearts grew afraid, and advised us clearly that we had gone far enough. It was just too strange, too Catholic.

We then noticed a door off to the right, and decided to try that. It opened to stairs, and we climbed up and up to the very top of the steeple, and gazed in hushed wonder out over the city and the harbour. I'm not sure I'd call it a religious experience, but it was more elevated than either of us had ever been before.

But there was trouble ahead! When we descended the stairs and stepped back into the vestibule, the worst possible thing that could have happened, happened. We found ourselves in the presence of a black-garbed Roman Catholic priest — an actual priest. It was sinister. We dropped our eyes and attempted to slide by him and out, but he walked toward us and spoke. When he asked if we were from the parish, we knew we were in trouble. I told him we were visiting from Summerside, hoping perhaps for diplomatic immunity, but then he asked my name.

Time seemed to stop.

I knew in that instant if I told him my name, it was all over. There were Protestant names and Catholic names. At twelve years of age I knew the difference, and I knew for certain he knew the difference. The moment called for boldness, so I screwed up my courage, looked him right in the eye, and informed him I was... David Gallant.

I was quite certain every single Gallant on Prince Edward Island was a Catholic, so it seemed a brilliant choice. Yes! David Gallant, the most rapid conversion since the experience of St. Paul on the road to Damascus, and it happened right there in the vestibule of St. Dunstan's Basilica. Thinking back I realize that the priest was probably quite friendly, but to one small Protestant boy from Summerside, it seemed I had just escaped the Inquisition.

Postscript

Thirty years later, on the five-hundredth anniversary of the birth of Martin Luther, I was invited to the Basilica to deliver a talk on the career of the great Protestant reformer. As my friend, Father James Kelly, introduced me, I reflected silently on the frightened boy in the foyer, and how much things had changed. I also wondered if perhaps there were any Gallants in the congregation.

The Mission

WE ALL UNDERSTAND TAXES, but there are fewer and fewer who understand tithing; that is, the obligation to set aside a percentage of one's yearly earnings for the work of the Church. Certainly there are fewer and fewer who practice it.

Years ago it was common for the Catholic parishes on the Island to bring in the "Brothers" once a year to conduct what was called a "Mission," and, from everything I've heard, the fires of hell were never closer, or hotter, than when those black-robed Redemptorist Brothers were on the scene. They would speak out vehemently against all the sins of the parishioners, real and imagined; and they would also raise money.

A man from up Tignish way told me about one witty old woman from his community who summed up the Mission in words which were unforgettable. "Oh! blessed angels," she said, "but it was a lovely Mission. When it was all over there wasn't a mortal sin — or a dollar bill — left in the entire community."

The Riposte

THE PRIEST IN THE community was a formidable figure, exercising vast influence over every aspect of the lives of his obedient flock. He was God's man on the scene, and his authority had to be taken seriously; however, every now and then someone would "talk back," providing amusement and silent satisfaction for the entire community.

The priest in Corran Ban had bought a big car, which raised the eyebrows of more than a few parishioners. Many thought it unseemly. At the same time, there was a local female parishioner who adorned herself with copious amounts of jewellery, and liked to "paint herself up like a barn door." One day after church, she was reprimanded by the priest. "The Virgin Mary didn't need all that jewellery to do good works," he said.

"Is that right," she responded tartly, "and perhaps Our Lord didn't need a car like yours to say Mass."

The Pope's Collar

AN OLD MAN LIVED alone in a house on St. Mary's Road, and, like many other old bachelors throughout the country, he lived mostly in the kitchen. The rest of the tumble-down house was of little use to him, except for the parlour where he stored his grain.

What the man was lacking as a housekeeper he made up for in his Catholic devotion. The structure was falling in around him, but crucifixes and religious pictures adorned the walls of every room.

One fall day some neighbours were helping him pile grain into the parlour. The old floor creaked and groaned and the men wondered how much weight it could stand. They voiced their concern but the old man reassured them. "Keep goin'," he said, "we'll be all right up to the Pope's collar."

At Great Length

SOME PEOPLE TOOK THEIR religion a bit too seriously, as was the case with an elderly woman named Eugennie, who was "wonderful to pray." At one local wake she led the entire gathering in an unending "prayer-a-thon," in which she diligently rhymed off the Rosary, the Litany of the Saints, the Litany of the Blessed Virgin, the Litany of the Sacred Heart, and followed this up with every prayer she could think of. When she could think of no more, she launched into the Stations of the Cross. She was about to embark on her Fourteenth Station when one old fellow at the back, eloquently expressing the worn patience and frayed nerves of the rest, boomed out authoritatively, "Mount Stewart next stop, get your grips."

Then there was the character from Launching who was part nuisance, part pontificator, part boozer, and part wit. He would have his pants up almost to his armpits and tilt his head back to drawl out his commentary, and though he wasn't especially funny much of the time, he worked at it — and occasionally got it just right. Once, when asked to comment on the priest's rather long-winded sermon, he pursed his lips and replied, "Well, he did pass by a number of good stopping places."

Our Bed

THERE WAS A PRIEST on the Island years ago who had a maid. When she talked about things in the rectory, she would always say, "my table," or "my stove." This irritated the priest and one day he told her, "The things in this house don't belong to you, so you should not speak of them that way. Your should say 'our' stove, or 'our' table."

A week later, the priest advised the woman that the Bishop was coming on business. "We will be in the study," he instructed, "and don't want to be disturbed by anyone."

The next day the Bishop arrived and the priest took him into his study and closed the door. Soon there was a knock. The priest ignored it, but after three or four more interruptions, he said to the Bishop, "I'd better see what it is. It must be something serious." He went to the door and opened it. There stood the distraught maid. "Father," she cried, "our cat just had kittens in our bed."

A Change I Suppose

A PROTESTANT MAN AND a Catholic man lived side by side, with just a fence between them. They got along famously most of the time, and did a lot of work together. But they never spoke on Sunday — not a word. It was, I'm sure, just a little convention to help them remember who they were.

One day the Protestant man up and died, and the day after the funeral the Catholic neighbour went across the field to see if there was anything he could do around the place. He met the widow in the yard, and told her how much he was going to miss Angus. She was touched.

"Yes, I miss him too," she replied, "but isn't it good to know he's in a better place."

The Catholic neighbour didn't say a word, just shuffled a bit and turned his cap round and round in his hands. The widow noted his discomfort. "Surely you believe he's in a better place?" she queried.

"Well," he replied softly, "it's a change I suppose."

Apples Tonight

DIRECT REFERENCE TO SEXUAL activity was not permitted in polite conversation; in fact, it was scarcely permitted in conversation at all. One woman from a rural area confessed that, in her circle, the act of sex was referred to arcanely as "apples." "That's right," she recalled, "when my husband was in the mood he would say, 'apples tonight!'" She didn't know the origin of the term, but I suspect it had something to do with the Garden of Eden, and the forbidden fruit of sexual passion. But, like everything else frightening or proscribed, the repressed topic invariably bubbled its way to the surface in the humour.

A couple, married for years, were attempting without much success to make love. The husband's attempts were, shall we say, rather flaccid. Finally, the long-suffering wife spoke up and said, "Perhaps the spark of life is gone." Her frustrated husband rolled over and snorted, "To hell with the spark of life. Trouble is your flue just don't draw anymore."

Years ago, in North Rustico, the community had gathered to honour one of its eldest residents, Eliza, who was celebrating her ninetieth birthday and was in remarkably good health — except for her partial deafness. It was a wonderful occasion, with many tributes to Eliza, and a good lunch. Various questions were asked about her life, and finally the master of ceremonies, in winding up the evening, asked, "Eliza, in all your life, have you ever been ill?" It was obvious she didn't get it, so the man decided to reword his question. Speaking more loudly he asked, "Eliza, in all your life have you ever been bed-ridden?"

Well, she brightened right up.

"Oh yes," she replied, "thousands of times. Twice in a dory."

Lord's Day Acts

THERE WAS THIS ONE family where the children all turned out bad, every one of them. One was an alcoholic, another in prison for embezzlement, and two who hid out in the parlour or upstairs because they were too "delicate" to face the world. There had to be a reason for such a sorry state of affairs, so there were some in the community who concluded it was because of the family's disregard of the Lord's Day.

For many Protestants on the Island, proper Sabbath observation was the litmus test of true piety. I am convinced that one of the reasons for this strict Sabbatarianism was that there was something wonderfully clear and attainable about it. You might not be able to keep your heart free of anger or lust, but, by God, with a little diligence you could keep the Sabbath free of work. It made you feel like you were getting somewhere.

There was one old bachelor from Glen Martin who was going blind and beginning to show signs of late-life confusion. One day he decided to go to Brooklyn for some long slabs he needed for one of his buildings. He walked the two miles and fetched what he required, but as he was nearing home he noticed, to his dismay, that his neighbours were on their way to church. It was the Sabbath, and he had forgotten.

What was he to do?

He turned around and carried the armful of slabs all the way back to Brooklyn. He would return for them Monday morning.

Another Sunday, a boy and his brother snuck their bicycles out of the shed and drove to the next community. They met an old gentleman who stopped them on the road. Like the reincarnation of Jeremiah, he cried out loudly, "Where are you boys from . . . hell?"

The Difference in James

AN ELDERLY MAN AND wife, whom we will call James and Myra, lived in a remote part of the countryside near Kensington. It was widely rumoured they enjoyed something less than an intimate relationship, and one day the doctor from Kensington discovered just how true those rumours were.

One morning he received word he was needed at their place. He knew neither of them was very well, but there hadn't been any calls for some time, so he was curious to see how they were getting on. When he arrived at the door, he was met by Myra. She informed him that he should perhaps have a look at James, who was lying on the lounge in one corner of the kitchen. The Doctor went over to examine him while Myra busied herself at the stove making tea for her guest. After a moment the Doctor stood up and said, "I'm sorry, Myra, but it appears James has been dead for some time."

"I knew there was something different about him," she replied flatly.

This Is My House

IN THE LONG COLD war that drags on and on between some husbands and wives, there are many border skirmishes. This is a story of one of them.

Birdie and Emmett got into a big row one night at supper. The more they tried to get out of it, the deeper in they got, until finally Emmett decided there was just one thing to do: he took off for the bootlegger's. That left Birdie with no way to vent her considerable anger, so she decided there was only one thing she could do: scrub the kitchen floor. My, what a cleaning she gave it; almost took the pattern right off the linoleum.

But it worked.

After a spell she started to feel a little better, and by the time she was finished she actually began to have some kindly thoughts about old Emmett. Putting away the bucket and mop she went to bed to await his return.

About eleven, the thoroughly hammered Emmett staggered into the house and slammed the door. Unfortunately, the trip to the bootlegger's hadn't done for him what scrubbing the floor had done for Birdie. A voice from upstairs called out sweetly, "Emmett darlin', take off your boots. I'm just after scrubbin' the floor."

"Shut your mouth," roared Emmett. "It's my house. I'll shit on the floor it I want to."

Silence.

Then a voice from above. "Well Emmett my dear, if that's what you decide to do, don't bother wipin' your arse. The undertaker will do it for ya in the mornin'."

THE HYPOCHONDRIAC

IN THE FIVE YEARS I performed the show, "A Long Way from the Road," one story that was a perennial favourite with audiences was the "Cake for the Wake" anecdote. What follows is a variant of that story from up-east.

There was a chap from near Souris who was a notorious drinker and a terrible hypochondriac. Every so often he would take to his bed — usually after one of his terrific sprees — and inform his wife he was sure he was dying.

This became more than a little tedious over the years, and there were days when his wife wished silently that his mournful predictions might come true. One day he was lying in the little room off the kitchen while his wife worked at the table, stemming berries for jam. At one point he called out for her, and she appeared at the doorway with a dish of berries in her hand.

"What is it now?" she asked impatiently.

"I don't think I'm going to make it," he informed her piteously.

"Well, you'd better tell me right now," replied the vexed wife, "because if you are I'm puttin' these in bottles, and if not, they're goin' in pies."

Mick McGuirk

THERE IS NOTHING SO characteristic of Island humour as the ironic quip or cutting remark. In a society of neighbours and relatives, where it is often difficult to be candid about one's feelings, negative emotion often found expression in biting one-liners, or acerbic, off-handed comments. It was sometimes called "dry" humour, but, more often than not, it oozed criticism.

There were many Islanders who perfected this ability, but surely one of the most accomplished was a man called Michael "Mick" McGuirk from Dromore. According to one story, Mick was delivering some potatoes to Government House. The Lieutenant-Governor at the time invited him into the kitchen for a wee drink before his trip back home. Mick was quite receptive to the hospitality and was handed the drink in a small glass. He took a polite sip, then asked his host if the glass was pressed or blown. The Lieutenant-Governor was a bit embarrassed. He said he really didn't know, but thought it was probably blown.

"Isn't it too bad," quipped Mick, "that the man who made it was so short of breath."

On another occasion, Mick was working in the field when the priest came up the road and stopped for a chat. Mick had recently completed the construction of a new chimney, which, it seems, was none too straight. He had already heard a few comments about it and was getting tired of the wisecracks. During their conversation, the priest asked, "And does the new flue draw well, Mick?"

"Yes Father," replied Mick, "it draws the attention of every damn fool who passes."

The stories of Mick's droll wit are many, but this is my favourite. Mick was in church one Sunday at St. Patrick's Church in Fort Augustus. The building was hot and a lady sitting ahead of him fainted and crashed down between the pews. The woman was very large and several men struggled unsuccessfully to dislodge her and get her into the aisle and outside. Mick, helping from the rear, was having rather a hard time getting a grasp anywhere. In the midst of it all he was heard to comment, “If only she had a butt of a tail it would be a big help.”

One Pile

ONE OF THE MOST important tasks of winter for many Island farmers was digging mussel mud. The lime-rich mud was extracted from the bottoms of bays and rivers through a hole in the ice, then hauled home on sleighs to be spread across the acidic soil of Island farms. It was brutally hard work, and desperate cold, but it was the mark of a good farmer to be diligent in the performance of this annual ritual.

Two men from up-west met on the road during the mudding season, and stopped for a chat. The older of the two was surprised to discover that the other man had not yet begun to haul. "You should be at it, Maurice," he advised brusquely.

"Oh I'll get around to it," Maurice replied nonchalantly.

"Well," retorted the older man, "you should be at it right now. If I was able I'd be at it. You wouldn't catch me this time of year not diggin'." He picked up the reins and prepared to leave, but paused for one last word. "I'd like to see all the mud I dug in one pile," he commented proudly.

"Yes," replied Maurice, "you musta dug a lot. I'm doubtful one pile would hold it."

So Much Like Himself

ISLANDERS ARE FAITHFUL IN their daily perusal of the death notices and great for going to wakes. I asked one man why he and his wife listened so religiously to the death notices on the radio every day at noon. "Oh!" he responded immediately, "that's how we find out where we're goin' that night."

And you never know what you're going to hear at a wake. You just never know. The remarks of two women were overheard as they came out the door of the funeral home. "My," said the first, "didn't he look good. So much like himself."

"And why wouldn't he look good," retorted the second, "he spent half the winter in Florida."

On another occasion, two men stepped into the viewing room at one of the local funeral homes. An acquaintance had been killed in a car accident and they had come to pay their respects. They removed their caps, walked to the side of the open coffin, and stood silently for a few moments, just staring at the remains. Finally, one of them broke the silence. "It's too bad," he whispered, "but one good thing about it, he wasn't badly hurt."

Too Much Wait

It runs counter to the stereotype, but the truth is there were many "laid-back" Islanders who just didn't like waiting for the ferry. Perhaps more than anything else the Bridge is a monument to impatience, and the modern cult of convenience. Waiting at the terminal was, for generations, an integral part of the experience of Islanders and their visitors. Some embraced it, and some endured it philosophically, while others resented the delay and experienced the wait on the pier as a denial of their personal right to freedom of mobility. In a word, it made them feel trapped. This was certainly true of a man some years ago who was attempting to escape at Wood Islands.

It was, by our standards, a blistering summer day, and this fellow from away was in a very long line-up, fuming over the delay. As the hours passed, both he and his vehicle became hotter and hotter, and eventually he managed to work himself up into quite a remarkable rage. He spotted a ferry worker standing near the side of the wharf, and marched over to vent his anger. "I'll tell you one thing," he concluded, "if I ever get off this goddamned Island I'm never, ever coming back." With that off his chest he wheeled around, stumbled over a hawser, and fell over the side into the water. The ferry worker looked down and watched as the man popped to the surface and thrashed his way to a nearby ladder. Then, as he clambered up over the side onto the pier, the worker drawled, "I see ya decided to come back after all."

Now's Your Chance

THIS STORY BEARS AN unmistakable resemblance to all those travelling salesman jokes that seem to enjoy a perennial popularity. However, it has been cleverly adapted to accommodate the unique circumstances of rural Prince Edward Island.

Years ago, a common figure on the little back roads of the Island was the pack peddler. He was quite a sight, trudging up the lane all weighted down with a huge backpack, and a suitcase in either hand. One late winter evening, in a remote part of the Island — which could have been most anywhere — a peddler arrived at a little house just at nightfall. Tired and hungry, he needed a place to bed down for the night, so asked the man and woman if he could put up with them. Well, they couldn't say no. There was a code of hospitality in the rural areas that just couldn't be broken: the visitor in need could not be turned away. But the woman was blunt with him. "It's been a long winter," she said, "and we're desperate short of supplies. All we have to eat are a few biscuits, but you're welcome to share them."

The peddler, realizing it was probably his last chance, took off his pack and sat down to the table. There were two biscuits on each plate, and a bit of molasses in a jar. And that was it. It didn't take him very long to finish those, and when he was done he looked wistfully toward the back of the stove at a bowl containing more biscuits. The man of the house saw him looking, and said, emphatically, "Those be for our breakfast."

When it came time for sleep, it turned out there was only the one bed in the place. The woman told the peddler he was welcome to share it, and though it seemed a queer arrangement, he judged it better than the barn, or the ditch. The old woman got in on one side; her old man, a heavy creature, crawled into the middle; and the peddler made do with what room was left.

In the middle of the night a terrible rumpus erupted somewhere in the vicinity of the barn. The man immediately crawled out of bed, pulled on his overalls, and went out to see what was the matter. Meanwhile, the woman and the peddler rolled together into the space he had vacated.

As soon as the man was out the door, the woman gave the peddler a poke in the ribs. "Now's your chance," she whispered seductively.

So he jumped right up and ate the rest of the biscuits.

Wooden Man

MANY YEARS AGO THERE was a man named John MacLeod who everyone in the community referred to as "Wooden." The man who told the story couldn't recall the reason for this nickname, but by the time he was finished I had some ideas of my own.

Wooden was well past boyhood and decided one day that it was time to find himself a wife. He looked around the community and saw a MacKay girl he liked. He persuaded her to go out with him, and they began courting, but as time passed Wooden realized he required the permission of her father before they could get married.

That was a problem. Wooden didn't have an especially good reputation around the community, and he felt it wasn't likely Mr. MacKay would give assent to their marriage. But he was a schemer and recalled the custom that you could send someone to ask in your place — someone highly esteemed. It seemed his only recourse, so Wooden begged a prosperous man in the community to carry his request. After some persuading, the man finally agreed and the two of them arranged a night to go to the MacKay farm.

When they arrived, Wooden was too scared to go in and said he would wait behind the barn. His emissary went to the door and knocked, and Mr. MacKay invited him in. After some few minutes of small talk the man announced the purpose of his visit. MacKay refused flatly. He did not, he said adamantly, wish to have that "conniving bastard" as a part of his family. And that was that.

When the man emerged from the house, Wooden came running out from behind the barn. "What did he say?" he asked hopefully. The man replied. "He turned you down. In fact, he said he would never allow a conniving bastard like you in the family."

"Well that must have made ya feel awful cheap!" replied Wooden.

The Second Funeral

A VERY LARGE WOMAN was being waked in her own home, and because of her immense size the coffin had to be made extra high and wide, and an extra handle added at each end. When the pallbearers were taking her out of the house, the coffin, being so large and cumbersome, kept hitting the door cases. After one especially hard bump, the "deceased" stirred, opened her eyes, and attempted to sit up. The pallbearers froze, and one man turned to the fella next to him and whispered, "What do we do now?"

The fat lady had not been dead at all, only in a coma. She revived completely and lived for almost another year. Her husband, of course, kept her over-sized coffin and the day of her second funeral the same men were hauling the same load out of the parlour and into the hallway. The somewhat intoxicated husband, following close behind, spoke out. "Go goddamn gentle, lads," he advised, "we don't want the same thing to happen as happened last year."

Droll

In every community there were tight-lipped individuals of droll temperament who were observers of the scene around them, but said very little. Silence was their sanctuary and they remained there most of the time; however, when they occasionally did venture forth, in brief utterance, it made the moment all the more dramatic — and humourous.

A young fella from Launching was obsessed with the idea of purchasing a car, and day after day regaled other family members with descriptions of his dream-machine. "I want something that'll squeal all the way from here to the Harbour," he declared enthusiastically.

His brother, terminally taciturn, chewed off this bit of advice: "Buy a pig."

On another occasion, in another community, a group of women were gathered for the evening around the hooking frame. The parish priest had recently died, and as they worked they spoke of him. One notoriously talkative creature was going on and on about how close the priest had been to her family. "Father Pat was Dad's best friend," she proclaimed proudly.

Another woman, without missing a loop, responded tersely, "Father Pat was everybody's best friend."

The Undercut

I CALL IT THE "undercut"; that is, the outwardly innocent comment that is intended to impale the listener on the sharp point of its hidden intent. It is most often used when someone is giving you grief.

A man from Prince County, who spoke with a stutter, worked on the roads most of his life, and in the winter drove the snowplow. One day a supervisor from the Department of Highways arrived to check on the performance of the workers in that area and was giving the man a hard time over a particular stretch of road he had plowed. The high-and-mighty supervisor went on for some time, telling him it wasn't wide enough, or neat enough, or straight enough. The snowplow operator endured this for about ten minutes, and when the man was finally finished, he asked, "H-h-h-how is it for length?"

Then there was the man from the Kilmuir area named Donald Doinkin, known to be close with a penny. When he went to MacGowan's Store he would always solicit a few free matches. This annoyed the staff, and one day when he asked, the clerk gave him two. Doinkin stared at the matches in his hand, smiled sarcastically, and asked, "Did ya mean to give me more than just the one?"

The Roundabout

CLOSELY RELATED TO THE "undercut" is what I call the "roundabout." It lacks the exquisitely fine stiletto-point of the undercut, but is, nonetheless, an insult once-removed.

Joe MacLeod, a blacksmith who worked out of Victoria, was a man well known for being sarcastic. One day a farmer came into his shop looking to get his horse shod. Joe noticed immediately that the animal was in frightfully poor condition. The man, of course, didn't want to admit he wasn't taking proper care of his horse, so he asked Joe, "Would you know of a good tonic I could give this horse to build him up?" Joe pushed his large wad of tobacco hard into his cheek and released a large spit across the fire. "Did ya ever try oats?" he replied.

Then there were the two neighbours who were sitting side by side at a funeral. The priest went on and on extolling the virtues and talents of the deceased, and at one point related that he had seen the man the day before he died, and that he was playing the fiddle. The two neighbours, who had known the dead man all his life, were finding the eulogy just a little rich for their blood. At the mention of the fiddle, one of them leaned toward the other and whispered, "All that he could play didn't kill him."

This calls to mind another story about the old fiddler in one community who was giving lessons to a young man whose desire to learn far exceeded his natural talent. For some months, the old man endured patiently the weekly agony of the lessons but saw little in the way of improvement. One day he just couldn't take it anymore. "Ronnie," he said, "why don't you give it a rest for a couple of weeks . . . then give it up altogether."

GETTIN' OUT THE VOTE

IT WOULD BE AN understatement to say that Islanders take their politics seriously, and one not raised in our political climate would have difficulty imagining the passion, zeal, and outright machinations of election-day activity. In any given election a higher percentage of Islanders turn out to vote than anywhere else in the country. By far. Most of us get to the polls on our own, but many are hauled there. Indeed, Islanders seem to think the Biblical adage, "Go out into the highways and byways and compel them to come in," is instruction for election day.

I recall being at the poll one election day as workers from both sides were bringing people to vote, some of whom hadn't been seen in public for years, or at least since the previous election. I was standing beside an acquaintance having a chat as a car pulled up with a frail old man and woman in the back seat. The worker opened the door and supported one on either arm as they made their tottery way into the polling station. My friend turned to me and quipped, "What is this anyway, election day or resurrection day?"

On another occasion, two workers of the same political persuasion were standing outside the door of the poll having a smoke. It was late in the day, and their work was finished. To their surprise, they saw a member of the opposing party go tearing off up the road in his car.

"Where's he goin'?" queried the first. "All the votes are in."

"He's off to the cemetery to fetch his father," the other man replied.

One poll chairman said he got the job one election of driving a mother and son to the poll, and that the young man was "none too swift." All the way to the poll he tried to drill it into the boy's head to put his mark on the lower line. "The lower line," he repeated again and again. Well, the mother voted and then the young man went behind the curtain. Soon he called out loudly, "Maaa, is it the upper line or the lower line? I forget." She, of course, couldn't say anything and a moment later he bawled out again.

"Just mark it, dear," his mother replied.

A moment later the boy came out looking frustrated and close to tears. "It's damn well marked now," he said.

That night when the votes were being counted there was, among the spoiled ballots, one with about ten X's marked from top to bottom.

Morning Ryan

Distinctions of class were of relatively little importance in rural Prince Edward Island, but in Charlottetown it was different. There were those there who fancied themselves members of the elite and expected to be acknowledged by others in a style appropriate to their elevated station.

A man named Ryan, an Irish Catholic, lived on Rochfort Street in Charlottetown in the 1880s. He was one of those who worked with his hands, and every Sunday morning after early Mass, if it was a warm day, he would change his clothes, go out and sit on the front step of his nice little frame house, and pass the time with those going by.

Every Sunday, at the same time, Edward J. Hodgson would pass by on his way to church. Hodgson was a member of the Establishment, an Anglican, and a man of considerable wealth who had become something of a power behind the scenes in Island politics. He would come by, all turned out for church with his tails and top hat, and his gloves and cane. When he would pass Ryan on his step, he would say, "Morning Ryan," and just as politely Ryan would reply, "Mornin' your Honour."

Now this went on for a long time — for years — and it was bothering Ryan more and more. One Sunday morning, he got up and went to his early Mass as usual and came back and changed his clothes. This day, however, he went out back to his little shed and got into a bottle of gin he had hidden there, then came back out and sat on the steps to wait for Hodgson.

Sure enough, at the appointed time Hodgson came by and as usual said, "Morning Ryan." Ryan swallowed hard and replied, "Mornin' Hodgson."

Mailman's Daughter

Some time ago, a woman wrote to me about an exchange she had overheard at a seniors' residence in Charlottetown. She captured the conversation so perfectly that I would like to relate it as described. I have, however, changed the names to prevent possible embarrassment.

Dear David,

It's important to find humour even in confusion, and so I'll share this conversation between two elderly women overheard at the Manor.

Lucy:	My father was a mailman.
Blanche:	Really? So was my father.
Lucy:	Is that so. My father delivered mail out around Hunter River.
Blanche:	I can't believe it. My father delivered mail there too.
Lucy:	So what was your father's name?
Blanche:	Duncan MacLean.
Lucy:	Oh for heaven's sake, that was my father's name too.
Blanche:	Maybe we're related.
Lucy:	Very likely.

The nurse then reminded them they were sisters.

Sincerely,
A Friend

Alex Isn't Home

Some people think it wrong to laugh at human frailty and weakness, or to make light of human distress. Those people don't understand humour. You show me a joke that has in it not the slightest trace of human frailty, and I'll show you a joke that has in it not the slightest trace of humour. Like it or not, that's just how it works. And now my story.

There was this man from Glen William whom everyone called "Stuttery Alex." He was unmarried and lived alone with his doddering old mother. One day he was going to Murray River to the store and told her, if anyone called, she was just to say, "Alex isn't home." He repeated the instructions several times and set off on his trip.

He arrived at the River only to discover he had forgotten his list, so used the pay phone at the garage to phone home and ask his mother what items he had marked down. But every time the operator would ring through, the old woman would pick up the phone and say, "Alex isn't home," then promptly hang up.

After trying several times, and becoming increasingly worked up about the money he was wasting, Alex decided he would try once more. As soon as he heard the click he blurted out, "It's d-d-d-damn well I know he's not home."

But it was too late. She was gone again.

The Explosion

CHILDREN LOVE FART JOKES, but I've observed that adults get quite a charge out of them, too. I know I do.

It was years ago, in Maximville. A family had returned from Boston for their annual summer visit with the relatives. One of the daughters had a stylish red silk dress, and there being no dry cleaning service in the area, she decided to wash it out in gasoline — which was, I'm told, a common practice. When she finished, she didn't know what to do with the leftover gas, but a cousin told her she might as well pour it down one of the holes in the outhouse. Which she did.

Also home from the States was a corpulent old uncle who always went to the outhouse after dinner to relieve himself and enjoy a smoke. Seated on one hole he lit his cigarette and threw the match into the other. There was a terrific explosion, which propelled the man off the seat and right out the door. He picked himself up and cleaned himself off. Determining that he had received no serious injury, he made his way into the house where he related the story to the greatly amused family. "I don't know what it was," he concluded, "must have been something I ate."

Hell's Bells

Some people are adept at expressing their anger. Others, as the old saying has it, "wouldn't say shit if their mouths were full of it." On Prince Edward Island, the eternal proximity of family, friends, and acquaintances inhibits the clear, voluble expression of rage. Most of us learned early to pull in our horns and to mute the voice of negative emotion in order to avoid nasty, long-term repercussions. It's possibly why practitioners of internal medicine in the province have so many patients.

Harold was one of those mild-mannered, church-going men who never had anything bad to say about anyone. He abstained from vulgar expression of any kind, and his occasional "hell's bells" was his deepest dip into profanity. One day, when he heard about an especially foul deed, he got so upset he said, "Hangin' is too good for him. They should . . . kick him in the arse."

Then there was the effete man from up-west who returned from a trip to Town sooner than expected and discovered the neighbour's boots in his porch. He went upstairs, opened the bedroom door, and discovered the man in bed with his wife. "What are you rascals up to?" he demanded.

A man from Launching worked on a building crew with a notoriously gentle and soft-spoken carpenter. Each day the man brought his beloved dog to the work-site and left it in the car with the windows rolled partway down. One day, in a devilish attempt to provoke him into profanity, one of his co-workers secretly fed the animal a snack he had laced with a powerful laxative. Naturally, the poor dog shit all over the inside of the car. When the owner went to check on his pet at the noon break, the rest of the crew loitered nearby in a state of concealed anticipation and excitement. The carpenter surveyed the scene of the natural disaster and finally exclaimed, "Dear, dear Tiger, you surely are a bad dog."

Not Too Bad

I DON'T THINK I'D be too far out on a limb to say Islanders are a careful breed; careful with our money, careful with our emotions, and especially careful with our opinions. Guarded, very guarded, that's what we are. Like good soldiers we don't like to put ourselves in a situation where there's no fall-back position.

One man was asked on a Sunday afternoon what he thought of the minister's sermon that morning. He shuffled and scratched his head, then replied, "It was all right, I suppose, but the people around me didn't seem to like it much."

Crafty!

There is a quality of prudence and circumlocution in the conversation of some Islanders that has been raised to a fine art form. In one community there were two competing general stores, and a local woman was asked which one she preferred. "Oh," she replied after brief hesitation. "I don't mind Trainor's."

This genius for evasion was also expressed in a story told me last summer from the Orwell-Eldon area. Apparently, the nephew of a couple who had just celebrated their fiftieth wedding anniversary arrived at the home of three bachelors who lived nearby. He asked them if they had gotten over to the celebration. "No," replied one of them, "it was too far to walk . . . and too close to drive."

I do believe that if there is any quintessential Island saying, it is the phrase, "not too bad." It captures perfectly the cautious, noncommital quality that pervades our culture. Whether it's a question about the weather, one's health, or the day's catch, the answer, more often than not, will be "not too bad."

And is this an accurate reading of the Island temperament? Well . . . not too bad.

Close to the Vest

THERE ARE TWO RULES of thumb that operate just below the surface in the conversation of many Islanders. The first is that, when possible, a person should always withhold information; and the second, like unto the first, is that one should never, under any circumstances, offer unsolicited information. The reason these unwritten laws operate so powerfully here is that what you don't say can't be held against you. But the result is sometimes infuriating.

One day Joe was driving his horse and wagon down the road when he met Peter, a man from the next community. When Peter saw Joe, he yelled out for him to stop. Now Joe wasn't an especially sociable type, but he pulled over as requested.

"Joe," inquired Peter, "didn't you have a horse with the heaves a spell back?"

"Yes," responded Joe.

"And what did you give her?"

"Kerosene," replied Joe, and drove off.

A week or so later the two men met again on the road, and once again Peter hailed Joe and motioned for him to stop.

"I thought you told me you gave your horse a dose of kerosene," said Peter.

"I did," replied Joe.

"Well I did the same thing and my horse died," related Peter.

"Mine, too," replied Joe, and drove away.

The Emergency Brake

ISLANDERS ARE, FOR THE most part, a conservative crowd. I don't mean in a political sense, though a few of them are that as well. I am referring rather to the innate caution that underlies the Island personality. We don't rush into things, and a significant change of any kind requires three years — one to think about it, one to plan it, and a third to be talked out of it by the rest of the family.

I am reminded of the story of the Mountie who was following an Island car down the highway. He noticed smoke billowing out from around the back wheels of the vehicle, so he pulled the man over to see what was wrong. After the usual terse exchange of greetings at the window, the Mountie looked in and noticed that the emergency brake was pulled on. It was an embarrassing moment for the driver, but his comeback was classic. "I always drive with it on," he said. "A fella never knows when he's going to get into a scrape."

Prickly Pride

In the rural areas, many of the old-timers lived a precarious existence. They were dependent on the elements, on their horses, on their neighbours, and, more than many of them cared to admit, on their wives. It was humbling, and the only way their egos could survive day to day was by presenting to the world a crusty, often prickly, pride.

A man from Bangor, William "Windmill" Compton, was such a man. He went one morning over to a neighbour's to borrow a tool. The neighbour was willing and went and fetched it out of the shed. Windmill thanked him and headed for home, but, as he was walking away, the man called out, "Be careful with that. The handle's worn pretty bad. It won't take much of a strain." Windmill stopped in his tracks, stood motionless for a moment, then walked back and placed the tool in his neighbour's hand. "I didn't want it that bad," he snapped, then turned and walked home. He would make do some other way.

Another Compton man, recently immigrated to the Island, built a new house in St. Eleanor's for himself and his wife. She remained in England until the construction was completed, and when she finally arrived, her husband proudly showed her their new home. Unfortunately, the house fell somewhat short of the woman's expectations, and the only feature of the dwelling that elicited a compliment was the doorknob. It was a terrible blow.

"Let's go!" said the husband.

"Where?" she asked.

"Out of here," he replied angrily.

Compton led his wife some distance from the house and told her to stay there. He then went back to the dwelling, retrieved the doorknob, and burnt the place to the ground.

They spent the winter under extremely harsh circumstances.

TOUCHY

SOME OF THE OLD people were desperate touchy, with a finely tuned ear for criticism. They could extract insult from almost any conversation, and the best of them could find reason for offense in a common greeting, if it wasn't delivered in just the right tone of voice.

There was this one fella named Johnnie who went over to the neighbour's to help out with the thrashing, but got insulted somehow and went home. The neighbour was at a loss to know what he had said or done, but, being cut from the same cloth, it was impossible for him to ask. The upshot of the incident was that they didn't speak — not a word — for three years. Then one day when they were both walking on the road, they came around a corner and found themselves face to face. "Good day, Johnnie," said the neighbour. "Yes," replied Johnnie, "good day for thrashin'," and kept right on going.

On another occasion, a man was being served lunch by a neighbour's wife. When he was finished, he complimented her several times on the scotchbread. When he left, the woman became visibly upset, and her husband asked her what was wrong.

"I guess he didn't think much of the rest of the lunch," she replied tautly.

Then there was the time the men of the parish were helping to build St. George's Roman Catholic Church in St. George's. Alex "Red" John MacDonald and his horse arrived around noon, and the priest asked him wryly how long it had taken him to get there.

"A half a day," replied Alex Red John, "and another half to go home." And left.

Sarcasm

THE WORD SARCASM HAS powerful etymological origins, being derived from two Latin words. The first is "flesh" and the other, "to rend." Most Islanders, of course, didn't understand Latin, but that didn't stop them from "tearing a strip" off someone when the situation called for it.

A man in Fort Augustus cut himself bad with the axe and was rushed by a friend all the way to Town for treatment. They arrived at ten past twelve, just as the Doctor was leaving his office for lunch. He was obviously none too pleased with the interruption of his noon plans, but he took the man inside and did the necessary suturing. When they emerged some time later, the concerned neighbour asked about his friend. The doctor said he would be fine, then proceeded to grumble some more about being called on during his lunch hour.

"Well I'm very sorry, Doctor," replied the driver. "I'd 'a brought him sooner but I had to wait for him to cut hisself."

THE STAMP

MANY OF THE STORIES told across the island were character-related, and could only be fully appreciated if you knew the individuals in question. Often the humour is lost when such stories are lifted out of this context of neighbourly familiarity. But not always.

It happened in Murray Harbour. A man named Carl Richards went into Howard Cohoon's store and asked him if he had found a ten-dollar-bill on the floor. He had been in the day before, he said, and thought he might have dropped it. Howard had indeed found the money, but, believing it had been dropped by a salesman, had sent it to him in the mail. He told Carl he would write the salesman and retrieve the money if he could. Some time later the money was returned, and Howard gave it back to Carl, who wanted him to keep half of it for his trouble.

Howard said he didn't want the five dollars — wouldn't take it — but asked if he could have the two cents for the second postage stamp he had used.

Hidden Bottles

For much of our history, this has been a society of barn-drinkers. There are more than a few of them left, but years ago drinking in the barn or the bait shed was the norm. Indeed, I know for a fact there were women married to terrible boozers who never once actually saw their husbands take a drink.

A man from Tignish loved to go to the horse races and to have his bottle of liquor at the track. His wife, however, was not supposed to know anything about this. One day, he and his buddies started out for the races, but a few miles down the road he realized he had forgotten his liquor book, which at that time was required to get a bottle from the liquor store. A few minutes after he had left, he barged back into the house. "Did you forget something?" asked his wife.

"My Rosary," the man replied. "You know how I hate to go anywhere without those beads."

Another man had hidden his liquor from his wife all through their marriage. When he died, he was being waked at home and a neighbour came into the parlour to discover the man's wife feeling around inside the coffin. "Mary," she said in surprise, "what on earth are you doing?"

"I was looking to see if there were any bottles hidden in here," she replied, "just to be sure he's dead."

Kitchen Politics

A FORMER LIBERAL MEMBER of the Legislative Assembly told me this story, which he has also shared in the Legislature and at various political meetings. It is of an exchange he witnessed between his father and mother when he was a boy. "It was a serious matter at the time," he related, "yet hilarious when I think about it now."

One day when he was about ten years old, his mother, an ardent Irish Catholic, was standing at the stove preparing supper. As she worked, she was lamenting to her husband the fact that their four oldest children, except for one, had married non-Catholics. "For my mother, almost at the point of tears, this represented a terrible failure on her part, a true source of guilt," he recalled.

His father was seated in the corner reading the paper while his wife went on and on about this grievous state of affairs. Toward the end of her sad commentary, he spoke up. In a serious and quiet tone he said, "Well, Mary, it's not so bad. At least they all married Liberals."

RANK POLITICS

MOST SUPPORTERS OF DEMOCRACY believe citizens should be permitted to vote as they choose, according to conscience. That view is not widely held on Prince Edward Island, although it is creeping in more and more. Most Islanders pay lip service to the abstract principle of a free vote, but in practice it seldom works that way. And as for your own conscience, that is largely pre-formed by family and community long before you reach the age of majority.

Mary, an Island girl from a Protestant family, showed promise at school and was sent to Prince of Wales College for a college education. After graduation, she left the Island for Western Canada, returning several years later to spend the summer with her family. But the visit did not go smoothly. The changes in "Modern Mary" were a source of deep dismay to her traditional father. One day, during a discussion about an upcoming election, he grew angry and said, "You've come back here wearing men's trousers, you talk like a man, and you have a Catholic boyfriend. All this I can tolerate, but for God's sake, don't vote Liberal."

The line between "Liberal" and "Conservative" was so clearly marked across childhood consciousness that, as an adult, it was extremely difficult to step over. You were raised in the ranks and were expected to stay there. A man called Captain Jimmie Breen was one of these "rank" Liberals. During one election, years ago, he went to Malpeque Hollow to vote because he owned property there.

When it came time for him to vote, he couldn't find his spectacles, so a local man offered the use of his. "No sir!" he said emphatically, "I will not vote through Conservative glasses."

Then there was the woman, a very strong Conservative, from a dyed-in-the-wool Tory family, who married a Liberal from

Bridgetown. He was as steeped in his political tradition as she was in hers, and the first election after their marriage he pleaded with her not to cancel out his vote. Later she was recounting this to a friend. "No, sir. I said. I will turn over with you in bed, but I will never turn over with you in politics."

Doctor Brehaut

I ALWAYS HEARD HIM referred to as "old Doctor Brehaut," and though he had been dead for many years when I moved to Murray Harbour, his name came up often in conversation. It was clear he had become something of a legend in the Murray River-Murray Harbour area. The folk down there praised his skills as a physician, and his willingness to go to his patients in any kind of weather. But the accounts also suggested a certain whimsical quality in the man, which made for good stories.

Apparently an old fellow informed the Doctor one day that he was afraid he was losing his hearing. "I can't even hear myself fart," he complained. Brehaut examined him, then went into his little back room and prepared a concoction of some kind. "Here," he said, "try this."

"Will it help me hear better?" asked the man.

"No," replied Dr. Brehaut, "but it will make you fart louder."

Norman's Reverie

NORMAN'S ROAD, WHICH TURNS off the Shore Road in High Bank, was named after Norman MacLeod, not because he was famous or anything, but just because he lived there, at the end of it. Actually, I guess you could say Norman was sort of famous — within his own small circle. He had the reputation for being something of a genius, with a photographic memory. He was a great student of Scripture, and apparently if anyone quoted a verse from the Bible he could tell them not only what book it was in, but what page it was on.

Norman also had the reputation of being notoriously absent-minded and sublimely unaware of what was going on around him. The mundane tasks simply could not hold his attention for long. Some days he would arrive in the house with a faraway look in his eyes carrying a bucket of grain, or a forkful of hay, and his wife would have to turn him around and point him back in the direction of the barn. At least that's what I was told.

One day Norman was digging a well with a man named Vere, who was twenty feet down in the hole with a crowbar and shovel, while Norman was perched at the top pulling up the stone in a bucket. There were, of course, intermittent waiting periods, and during one of these Norman drifted off into a reverie. He shifted his position and a large rock tumbled down the pile and into the well, causing him to blurt out, "Run Vere! Run for your life!"

Brain Drain

Every generation we fatten and educate a very large number of our young people for emigration, and it's a common thing to hear Islanders speak of how we export so many brains. Sometimes we even brag about it. Mind you, we import some as well, but most Islanders seem to think we suffer from a trade imbalance.

One young fellow told me a few years ago about an old relative of his, a grand-aunt, if I remember correctly, who had never left Prince Edward Island — never set foot on foreign soil. Whatever kind of life she had, she had it here. All of it. When she was an old woman, she developed a rare brain disease, which eventually caused her death. As part of the post-mortem routine, her physician sent a slice of her brain to a laboratory somewhere in the United States. This prompted one of her relatives to comment with some indignation, "Imagine, all her life she never even thought of leavin', and now they've gone and shipped her brain to the States."

It seemed a great betrayal.

Born Away

I WAS TOLD THIS story last year by a man from Summerside. It sounds just a little too "on the nose" to be factual, but it made me laugh, and that seems a good enough reason to include it. Many of the stories in this little volume are not altogether factual. Some of them may never even have happened, at least not in the way they are recorded. But they are all, nonetheless, perfectly authentic.

He was from the Tignish area, and when his mother was expecting him she took a trip to New Brunswick to visit some relatives. It was in the late 1800s when there was a ferry that ran from Summerside to Pointe de Chêne. While she was away, she went into labour and delivered her son, a happenstance that affected the boy the rest of his life.

A week after his birth he was taken back to his Island home where he dwelt, without ever leaving, for the next ninety-eight years. Despite the fact he had never actually set foot on any other soil, he was teased all his life about not being an Islander. When he died, there was the usual information on his headstone, but someone scratched in at the bottom: SO LONG STRANGER.

The Tenth Load

IT'S AN AWFUL SHAME to erode a young man's spirit by the withholding of praise, yet near as I can tell this happened routinely on many farms. There was just no pleasing some of the old-timers, and many of them didn't believe in praise. Felt it had a corrupting influence.

About fifty or sixty years ago there was a young man who was cutting and hauling out wood for a neighbour, working with his brother with axes and a cross-cut saw from early morning until dark. For this they were receiving a day's pay of sixty cents apiece. One day, between the two of them, they cut and delivered to the house nine very large loads, each representing near a cord. They knew it had been an especially good day and were rightfully proud of their accomplishment. While they were having supper, their employer commented, "Too bad ya didn't start a quarter of an hour earlier. You might have gotten the tenth load."

WIPE-OUT

THE YEAR 1935 IS memorable in Island politics, especially for Liberals. In the election on July 23, the Grits, led by Premier Walter Lea, won every seat in the province. It was more than a landslide; it was a total wipe-out. The political landscape, like the soil itself, had turned entirely red, and ardent Tories across the Island were stunned.

A woman from Murray River was informed by her mother about the events of that election night. Apparently she and a friend went down to the Telephone Office in the village to wait for the election returns. They were true-blue Conservatives, and when the results came in they could scarcely believe it. It was their worst nightmare come true, and they were devastated. As they were walking home across the bridge, they stopped and gazed over the side into the darkness below. After a heavy silence, one of them said to the other, "Faye, that water looks some good."

That same evening, in Morell, a Conservative man commented to a friend about a recently deceased political ally. "Isn't Frank lucky to be dead," he said seriously.

Election Day Treats

Political patronage is endemic in this province — as Island as spruce leaning over the bank. It takes many forms, but one of the least pernicious is the time-honoured practice of bribing people on election day. I know it sounds pretty bad, but I don't believe it actually interferes very much with the democratic process. For one thing, both major parties do it, and, for another, it seldom affects the way people vote. After all, Liberals for the most part "treat" Liberals, and Conservatives Conservatives. If I were to be strictly Machiavellian about it, I would say the parties should give it up, not because it's corrupt, but because it doesn't work. On the other hand, it would entail the loss of some great stories.

An elderly gentleman, I think from the Wheatley River area, recalled a brilliant election day strategy he witnessed in his youth. He said that one party had given one of their supporters a pint to vote in his usual way. The other party, realizing the man could never actually bring himself to vote for them, offered him two pints to stay home.

The practice of "treating" is far less common today than it was years ago, when it was standard party procedure to bring in whole box-cars of election booze, and put aside a stash of crisp new five-dollar-bills for the teetotallers. During that era there was a certain family that could be swayed to vote either way, depending on the amount of money offered them. Even at that time it seemed a bit crass, and one election year both parties conspired not to get involved in a bidding war over the family's votes. It was collusion clear and simple, but it didn't work, for neither party trusted the other.

The night before the election the Liberals decided to pay the family a visit. They believed the Conservatives might not uphold their end of the deal, and they were right. Later in the evening, after the family had gone to bed, the Conservative delegation arrived. As they stood knocking at the front door, they looked up and saw the old man of the house, his head stuck out an upstairs window. "Too late," he exclaimed, "all bought and paid for."

African Odyssey

THE PERSON WHO RELATED this story was a bit hesitant about telling it. He reasoned, however, that since the character in question had been "dead for years," it might be all right for him to proceed.

It seems a group of men from the community had gathered to help a neighbour raise the roof of his barn. Included in the group was one fellow who was well known for his exaggerations. There was nothing he wouldn't say to make a good story better, or to enhance his reputation as a man of the world.

The men got talking about the interesting places they had visited. Several had been to the States and entertained the others with accounts of the strange and unusual sights they had seen there. Feeling left out, the man in question piped up and told everyone that he had been to Africa. He spoke of all the animals he had seen, but confided that he didn't much like the look of the women there. "You couldn't get near them anyway," he added, "too many old black bucks around."

One of the other men decided he would try him out by asking him how he had gotten there. "Well," he replied, "I went by boat, but I was that seasick I took the train back."

G'DAY

MOST ISLANDERS EXCHANGE INNUMERABLE greetings in the run of a day, and it's not just because we especially like one another. That's part of it, but it has at least as much to do with what people will think if one disdains this common civility. Whether on the sidewalk, or on the highway, you neglect greeting others at your peril. After all, who wants to be thought of as stuck-up, or big-feelin'. I lived for several years in Murray Harbour, and down there you wave at everyone, whether you recognize them or not — just in case. After all these years, I still wince when I think of all the times I forgot.

A well-known Island businessman, a most gregarious individual, was attending a meeting in Toronto, staying on the tenth or eleventh floor of a large downtown hotel. Now this is a man who seems to know everyone, and greets everyone — and expects to be greeted. As the story was told to me, he got up the first morning he was there, stepped on the elevator, and headed down to his breakfast appointment. As the elevator stopped on the various floors, and people stepped in, he greeted each one of them.

"Grand day!"

"How are ya now?"

But no one responded. Not a word. Just looked at him as if he was deranged. So when he arrived at the mezzanine level, where his breakfast meeting was scheduled, he stepped outside the elevator, turned to the crowd inside, and said with feeling:

"Yuh's can all go to hell!"

TEA

MANY OF THE OLD people were heavily addicted to tea. They liked it hot; they liked it strong; and they liked it often. The teapot sat on the stove from morning 'til night, and no meal or lunch was considered complete without at least one or two cups. One elderly Island woman from Freetown said her great-grandmother's most prized possession was her teapot. The story in the family is that when she emigrated from Scotland in 1856, she held her beloved teapot on her knee all the way across the stormy North Atlantic. Another Islander said that he could not remember a day in his life when he did not have his tea. "It would be like going without air," was how he put it.

Every winter there was a group of men who went deep into the woods by horse and sleigh to cut firewood for the next winter. At noon they would make a fire, melt some snow in a kettle, and make tea for their lunch. This one day a man named John opened his lunch, only to discover his wife had forgotten to put in the tea. He got up calmly, went over to his horse, and unhitched it from the half-loaded sleigh. When the others asked him where he was going, he replied, "Sufferin' hell, where do you think? I'm goin' for my tea."

Dear

I DON'T KNOW HOW others feel about it, but I rather like it when someone calls me "dear," and on Prince Edward Island that still happens a lot. I get it at the grocery store, at the bank, and at the liquor store, from people I know, and from people I don't. Mostly it's from women, but not always.

One woman, unacquainted with the custom, told me about the time she and her husband moved to the Island about thirty years ago. They were fixing up an old farmhouse in Brudenell and had hired a local plumber to help them put in a new bathroom. When he left on his dinner break, the woman went to her husband and said, "I don't know whether I should mention this or not, but that man's been calling me 'dear' all morning."

"Don't worry about it," replied her husband, "he's been calling me dear all morning, too."

FASTER PLEASE

FOR AS LONG AS human beings have crawled the face of the earth, there has been a powerful drive in the species to accelerate mobility. From the first hoisting of a sail, or the first rough ride on the back of a horse, "faster is better" has been our credo. On the Island we plunged ourselves into debt and changed our political destiny in order to build a railway; displaced the beloved horse to make way for the tractor and automobile; and scuppered the ferry service in order to build ourselves a Bridge.

The romantics have always protested such changes and have been quick to point out the shortcomings of the newfangled replacements. An anti-Fixed Link stalwart was asked recently about his first trip across the bridge to the mainland. "It doesn't even seem like a trip anymore," he replied morosely, "first thing ya know and you're there."

In the early years of the automobile, when the deeply rutted roads were often virtually impassible, and it was nothing to blow out two or three tires on a short trip, a woman was walking to Town. A car pulled up beside her and the driver asked if she would like a ride. "No thanks, Tom," she replied curtly, "I'm in too much of a hurry."

On another occasion, Father Patrick Doyle was taking the train to Tignish, which was near his home community of Palmer's Road. It was a slow trip with a stop every few miles to off-load passengers and freight. The good Father was doing considerable grumbling about all this, and the conductor finally asked sarcastically, "If you're mindin' the stops so much why don't you get off and walk?"

"I can't," quipped the priest, "they're not expectin' me that soon."

First Night

Sex for the new bride and groom was often traumatic. It was not uncommon for the young couple on their honeymoon to climb under the covers in a state of pure ignorance, without ever having had so much as a conversation about sex with anyone in their entire lives. One woman put it like this: "There was no sex education. Oh my, no! You just picked it up, and sometimes you picked it up wrong." Another woman related that she had "some inkling" of what married couples did but confessed that she was terrified by all she didn't know. She was seventeen when she married, and when she and her husband, eighteen, arrived at the hotel room for their first night together, she promptly locked herself in the adjoining bathroom to dress for bed. The duration of her stay was so lengthy that her youthful husband eventually tapped on the door and inquired nervously if everything was okay.

"It was the hardest thing I ever done in my life," she related, "to walk out of there dressed in my nightgown."

It seems the young man was also under considerable stress, for when she appeared at the door he took one look at her and immediately began bleeding profusely from the nose. As they attempted together to stanch the flow of blood, the young woman queried, "Will this always happen?"

Red, Green, and Orange

There is an entire generation grown up on the Island today who know little or nothing of the ancient feud between Irish Catholics and the Protestant Orangemen. This story won't make a bit of sense to many of them, but most of their grandparents will get it.

Years ago there was a priest from the Kelly's Cross/Kinkora area named Father Willie Monaghan. Like many priests at that time, he did a bit of farming on the side — even kept a couple of race horses. He is also remembered for his ready humour. One day when he was planning a trip to Charlottetown, a parishioner, an Irish Catholic like himself, asked if he could catch a ride in. Father Monaghan agreed and the two of them set off. When they arrived in the City they encountered something the parishioner had never seen before: the first set of traffic lights on the Island, at the corner of Elm Avenue — now University — and Euston Street. They stopped on the red, then pulled through on the green. The parishioner was greatly intrigued by this, and asked Father Willie to explain.

"Red means the French fellas can go through," replied the witty priest, "and the green is to let the Irish fellas through." His passenger, still in a state of amazement blurted out, "They don't give the Orangemen much time, do they?"

Badness

Most of the old people were firm believers in corporal punishment for children; that is, punishment that was administered directly to some part of the child's anatomy. A good swift kick in the arse or swats to the side of the head were considered indispensable to proper discipline, and parents who neglected such administrations were liable to be considered negligent or squeamish. It was widely believed that virtue could be beaten in, and badness beaten out, which says a lot about the view of human nature that prevailed at the time.

The efficacy of this approach to child-rearing was little questioned, though the evidence sometimes pointed in the other direction. An elderly woman was recalling two brothers from her community who were always up to some kind of badness. "I don't know why," she puzzled, "their father certainly used to take the belt to them enough." She paused, then added, "But they grew up to be nice men."

A certain young man was repeatedly warned by his father not to run the horses. One day on the way home from the field in the dump-cart, the boy could not resist giving the horse a good slap across the rear end with the reins. The animal bolted across the field, the cart bouncing up and down crazily among the furrows. He finally got the horse stopped but was badly frightened by the ordeal.

His father, having observed the entire episode from the barnyard, came running across the field. "Are you hurt?" he called out.

"No," replied the shaken son.

"That's good," replied the father as he continued toward the boy, "but you're going to be soon."

FATHER DOYLE

HIS NAME WAS PATRICK Doyle, Father Patrick Doyle, from Lot Seven, and he was one of those rare individuals who was able, by some special grace, to rise above the prevailing religious prejudices of his time. In an age on Prince Edward Island when the flames of religious intolerance were being fanned and stoked by many clergy, Protestant and Roman Catholic alike, he was a beacon of goodwill. Born in 1839, years before Vatican I, he breathed the irenic spirit of Vatican II.

Doyle was a man of many gifts, not the least of which was his ready wit. On one occasion, when he was the parish priest in Summerside, he was approached by some Methodists who were collecting for the construction of a new church. They knew of his openness and asked him for a contribution. According to the story as I heard it, Doyle reacted with mock horror. "Oh no," he replied, "I can't do that. It would be a great sacrilege for me, a Roman Catholic priest, to give money for the building of a Protestant Church!"

Just when his visitors were thinking they had made a great mistake, he smiled and added, "But I'll tell you what I can do. Here's ten dollars to help tear down the old one."

One winter day the Bishop was visiting Father Doyle at his rectory. As they chatted, Doyle noticed it was getting cold and excused himself to go put more coal on the fire. The Bishop, rather than staying put, followed Father Doyle down the stairs, and as they descended he noticed a rather long line of empty whiskey bottles on a shelf above the stairway. "Father," he commented dryly, "I see a lot of dead soldiers there on the shelf."

"Yes, Excellency," replied Doyle, "that is true. That is certainly true. But I want to assure you they all had a priest with them at the end."

There was a certain daring in Doyle's humour, especially in what we might refer to as his "ecumenical wit." By making light of what was so often grimly concealed, he provided an outlet for the pent-up anxiety associated with Catholic-Protestant relations on the Island. It's why his stories have been told and retold for more than a hundred years.

One day when Father Doyle was driving through his Vernon River parish, he stopped to give a lift to a stranger walking along the road. He introduced himself, and the stranger, in turn, said his name was Murphy. Doyle expressed surprise at this and commented that he had never seen him at Mass. The man proceeded to explain that he was from a neighbouring community and that, despite his name, he was a Protestant. They continued on their way, chatting amiably, until the man indicated he had reached his destination. As he stepped down from the buggy, Father Doyle said, "Mr. Murphy, could I give you a word of advice."

"Why, certainly," replied Mr. Murphy.

"Well," commented Doyle, "when it comes your time to leave this world, and you reach those great pearly gates, and when St. Peter asks you who you are . . . just tell him your name is Murphy and leave it at that."

Those Whitemen

IT COULD BE SAID that the native people of the Island, the Mi'kmaq, haven't had a lot to laugh about these past three or four hundred years. The opposite, of course, is true. There has been much they've needed to vent in their humour, and most of the ones I know love to laugh.

One prominent Mi'kmaq man often tells the story of the two native men who were standing off to one side observing the actions of a priest. It was during the early days of colonization when the European clergy, often to the amusement of the native people, were attempting to convert the Mi'kmaq to the "true" faith. Apparently, the priest took out a handkerchief, blew his nose, then returned the cloth to his pocket. At that point one of the bemused native men leaned over to his companion and remarked sardonically, "We'll have to watch out for those Whitemen, they want to keep everything."

Stock Exchange

The old horse trader, with a trained eye for strengths and defects, would walk around an animal the way a car salesman walks around a vehicle. There was no hood to peer under, but hooves were lifted, and lips stretched back, as he made his savvy assessment. And if he was good at his trade, he knew just when to buy, and when to sell.

There was one old trader from the Belle River area who was renowned for his bartering skills. It was nearly impossible to get the best of him, and it is alleged that one morning he left home with an animal, traded all day around the countryside, and came home that night with the very same horse and fifty-five dollars in his pocket.

Another trader bragged that one morning he took an old horse and set of harness to Miscouche and exchanged them for two holstein calves, a pair of rubber boots, and a quart of rum. "The same day," he continued, "I sold the calves in Sherbrooke to two separate farmers for two hundred dollars, drank the rum on the way home, and wore the rubber boots for years."

Another horse trader from the Murray Harbour area — I think it was Nelson Buell — was out at Guernsey Cove attempting to sell a horse to Ev Harris. He praised the animal up to the skies, so much so that Ev asked him why he would part with such a great horse for such a reasonable price. "Well, I'll just tell ya," Nelson confided, "the world is goin' at too fast a clip for a horse."

HOLD THE MEAT

AS PROTESTANTS WE HAD our own, perfectly reasonable, religious customs, but fasting wasn't one of them. That was something the Catholics did, and because we viewed it from the outside it seemed quite incomprehensible, even absurd. What could refusing to eat hot dogs on Friday, or giving up pop and chocolate bars for forty days, have to do with religion? Obviously nothing, and the only logical conclusion was that the Catholics had been too long under the thrall of popes and priests and could no longer think for themselves.

I also discovered at around the age of fifteen that Catholic fasting entailed more than food. I had a Catholic girlfriend at the time who informed me one evening that she was giving me up for Lent. Perhaps I should have been flattered, for I knew that Catholics only gave up those things which were a source of pleasure, but I really hadn't expected to be anyone's penance. I suppose it served me right for hanging out with the wrong kind.

When I was in grade ten at Summerside High School, an older girl, one of the goddesses in grade twelve, let it be known somehow that she was giving up French-kissing for Lent. I never forgot that; and the reason that I never forgot was that, being strictly Protestant, I didn't even know what it was, though I suspected it had something to do with the Acadian boys from the West End. What was clear was that Catholics couldn't be trusted. They just weren't logical.

One day, during harvest, a Protestant farm wife prepared an elaborate roast beef dinner for the men in the field. It was Friday and she had forgotten that one of the workers that day was George, a huge Catholic lad with an enormous appetite. As the crew sat down to the table, it dawned on her and she apologized to him. "It's all right, Pearlie," George replied as he piled his plate high with potatoes. "I can take the gravy, I just can't take the meat."

Now where's the logic in that?

On another occasion a Catholic man got into a fight at a dance and almost bit his adversary's ear off. He was bragging about it a few days later and boasted, "If it hadn't been Friday, I'd of chewed him right down to the heels."

The Calls

THE OPERATOR IN HUNTER River often became exasperated with a woman who had the habit of going to parties and getting quite drunk while her children were left at home to fend for themselves. The kids would put calls through to the house where the party was happening, begging their mother to come home. One night there were several such calls, which the distressed operator was obliged to put through. She wasn't supposed to listen in, but she did.

"When are you coming home?"

"Soon, dear."

Then later: "Are you coming home soon. The fire is out and wc'rc cold."

"Yes dear, right away."

Still later, at about one o'clock: "Mommy, please come home. The baby is crying."

By that time, the compassionate and increasingly worked-up operator had taken all she could take. "You fly to hell home to your kids or I'm calling the Child Welfare," she blurted.

And that was the end of the calls.

The Lemon Caper

THERE WERE THESE TWO guys from the St. Peter's area who got into the lemon one evening. They partied through the night and after daybreak decided to go back to the Bay and get some more extract. The fella driving fell asleep at the wheel as they were going down the Bay hill, and his companion, an extremely reserved, non-intrusive individual, couldn't bring himself to shout out, or shake him awake. He knew they weren't going to make the turn at the bottom but it was so against his nature to interfere that he sat looking straight ahead as they drove into the Bay and came to a stop in about three feet of water.

Frank Quigley came along and saw the accident. He stopped and shouted, "Can I do something for you?"

Now the passenger in the half-immersed vehicle had recently bought some shingles from Quigley that hadn't been delivered, so, standing there, dripping wet, he called back, "Oh yes, Frank, when are you going to bring up those shingles?"

Come On, Come On

About seventy years ago, there was an old man and woman, husband and wife, who lived in a small Acadian community. The old man was almost blind and all crippled up with rheumatism, and when they would be walking somewhere together on the road, the old man would invariably fall behind. When that would happen, his wife would turn and say, with some impatience, "Come on. Come on!"

In the winter of 1927, during an outbreak of the flu, the old woman fell ill and died. On the day of her funeral came a big snowstorm, and the Mass had to be cancelled. That very night the old man died. They were buried together two days later.

Over the next few weeks the coincidence of the two deaths was, understandably, the topic of much sentimental conversation in the community. One neighbour, recalling the old couple, commented, "Yes, it was just like on the road. Can't you just see her on the other side, lookin' back and sayin', 'Come on. Come on!'"

So Far from Everything

WHEN VISITORS COME TO the Island, most feel they are away from the centre of things, equating "offshore" with remoteness. That is an understandable point of view for mainlanders. They are, after all, away from their centre, wherever that might be. Islanders, however, have quite a different perspective. As absurd as it might sound, for many of us here, the Island is the centre — the "Still point of the turning world." This is no satellite. It is home base.

A tourist was strolling down the wharf at Tracadie Harbour. It was one of those brilliant, late summer afternoons, with the sun broken into a million pieces on the face of the bay. A fisherman was just after crawling up over the edge of the wharf, and the tourist attempted to strike up a conversation. "You're a fortunate man to live in such a beautiful place," he said.

"Suppose I am," replied the fisherman, "least that's what everyone tells me."

The conversation continued for a spell and eventually the fisherman asked the visitor where he was from.

"Atlanta," he replied.

The fisherman knitted his brows. "Atlanta?"

It soon became clear the Island man had little knowledge of this place called Atlanta, which, of course, greatly surprised the visitor.

"Why, Sir," he said. "Atlanta is a major city, of several million people, about fifteen hundred miles from here."

"Well now," responded the fisherman, "isn't that somethin' else. So many people, and them so far away from everything."